Contents

A Note About the Author

Charles Dickens is one of the greatest English writers. He was born near Portsmouth, in the south of England, on 7th February 1812.

Charles Dickens' father worked in an office. John Dickens did not earn much money and the family was poor. John Dickens could not pay the bills. When Charles Dickens was 12 years old, John Dickens and most of his family went to prison. Charles did not go to prison. He went to work in a factory. He had to work many hours each day. Charles Dickens was very unhappy at this time. He never forgot about his life at the factory.

In 1827, Dickens was 15 years old. He went to work in an office. He was not paid much money but he had many friends.

In 1833, Charles Dickens started writing stories. He became rich and very famous. *A Christmas Carol* was published in 1843. Other famous books by Charles Dickens are: *Oliver Twist* (1838), *Bleak House* (1853), *A Tale of Two Cities* (1859), *Great Expectations* (1861) and *Our Mutual Friend* (1864).

Dickens knew how the poor people lived in England. Many of his stories are about poor people. He wanted everyone to know how poor people lived. Many of the laws of England were changed after his books were published.

Charles Dickens died on 9th June 1870. He was 58 years old. Dickens is buried in the famous church, Westminster Abbey, in London.

A Note About Life in England in the Nineteenth Century

A *Christmas Carol* takes place in London in the 1820s. At this time, Great Britain was a very rich country. London was the largest city in Europe.

Many rich people lived in London. They had expensive houses and they had the very best food and drink. They travelled in fine carriages pulled by horses. They wore beautiful and fashionable clothes.

Charles Dickens lived in London. He saw how the rich people lived. But he also saw that thousands of poor people lived in London. They lived in small, dirty houses. They did not have enough to eat.

Many poor people could not get work. Men, women and children often became criminals. They stole food and clothes. Sometimes they killed people to get money. If a family could not pay their bills, they had to go to prison. The prisons in Britain in the nineteenth century were the worst in Europe.

England is divided into counties. And each county is divided into parishes. In the nineteenth century, officials of the parish looked after poor people. A workhouse was built in every parish. Workhouses were places where poor people had to live. They were usually terrible places. The poor people who lived in workhouses were given food and a bed. But they had to work very hard and the food was very bad. Many people died in workhouses.

1
Ebenezer Scrooge

It was three o'clock in the afternoon on the day before Christmas – Christmas Eve. In the city of London it was very cold and almost dark. But it had been almost dark all day. There was no sunlight because it was winter and it was very foggy. It was possible to hear people and horses and carriages. But it was not possible to see them because the fog was so thick.

Two names were painted on the door of an old building in the centre of the city: Scrooge and Marley. Jacob Marley had died seven years ago. But Ebenezer Scrooge had left Marley's name on the door of the building. Scrooge answered if people called him Scrooge and he answered if people called him Marley.

Scrooge did not care what people called him. Scrooge did not care about people. Scrooge cared about one thing – money! He worked very hard all the time and he earned lots of money. But he did not like spending money.

Ebenezer Scrooge was an old man. His face was thin and his nose was long and thin. His hair, eyebrows and whiskers were all white. Scrooge never smiled.

He had no friends. Nobody visited his house. Nobody said hello to him as he walked along the street. No beggar stopped him in the street and asked him for money. No dog went near him.

But Scrooge wanted his life to be this way. He did not like people. He liked writing down amounts of money in his account books.

2

Visitors for Scrooge

On Christmas Eve, Scrooge was working in his office. He was writing in his account books. He was writing down amounts of money people had paid him. And he was writing down amounts of money people owed him.

It was cold outside, but the fire in the fireplace was very small. The door of Scrooge's office was open. Scrooge could see into the next room, which was very small, and very cold too. The fire in the next room was even smaller than Scrooge's fire. One tiny piece of coal was burning in the fireplace.

Bob Cratchit worked in this small room. He could not have a bigger fire because Scrooge kept the coal in his own office. And Scrooge would not let Bob have any more coal.

'If you take any more coal, Bob Cratchit,' said Scrooge, 'you will lose your job!'

So Bob continued to write letters for Scrooge. He put his scarf round his neck and sat very close to the flame of his candle. Bob told himself that the candle was warm and it would make him warm. But that wasn't true!

Suddenly someone opened the front door. A young man came in from the street. He looked happy and cheerful. His eyes were bright and his face was red because of the cold. He shouted cheerfully, 'Hello! Merry Christmas, Uncle!'

'Nonsense! Rubbish!' replied Scrooge. 'Christmas is nonsense. It's humbug! Bah!'

'You don't mean that, Uncle,' said the young man.

'Oh yes I do,' replied Scrooge. 'Why are you cheerful? You don't have much money.'

'Why aren't you cheerful, Uncle? You've got lots of money,' said his nephew.

Scrooge couldn't think of an answer, so he repeated, 'Bah! Humbug!'

'Don't be angry, Uncle,' the young man went on. 'It's Christmas.'

'People who say "Merry Christmas" are stupid idiots,' said Scrooge. 'They said "Merry Christmas" last year. Now they are a year older and they have spent a lot of money and they say "Merry Christmas" again. They are idiots. I wish someone would cook them and then eat them for Christmas dinner!'

The young man was Fred, the son of Scrooge's sister, Frances. Frances had died many years ago. So Fred was Ebenezer Scrooge's only living relative. Fred was married to a pretty young woman. He was a kind and friendly young man. He liked people, so he went on talking to his uncle.

'Christmas is a very important time of year,' he said. 'People are kind and helpful to each other at Christmas. They forgive each other for all the bad things they have done. They help poor people. I feel happy at Christmas. I like Christmas.'

'Oh, yes! Yes! I agree!' Bob Cratchit said suddenly, from the cold little room.

'If you say one more word, Bob Cratchit,' shouted Scrooge, 'you will lose your job. And you mustn't say anything more either, nephew! Goodbye!'

'Oh, Uncle,' said Fred, smiling at the old man, 'I want you to have dinner with me and my family tomorrow.'

'If you say one more word, Bob Cratchit,' shouted Scrooge,
'you will lose your job.'

'Goodbye,' replied Scrooge loudly.

'I want you to have a happy Christmas with me and my family,' the young man said.

'Goodbye,' said Scrooge again.

At last the young man opened the door to leave. But he was still cheerful.

'Merry Christmas, Uncle,' he said. 'And Merry Christmas to you too, Bob.'

'Merry Christmas, sir,' replied Bob Cratchit. He smiled and waved.

'Bah!' said Scrooge to himself. 'Bob Cratchit is a poor man. He earns fifteen shillings a week. He has to buy food for his wife and six children and he is talking about a merry Christmas. Everyone is mad – completely mad!'

As Scrooge's nephew left, a gentleman came in. He went into Scrooge's office.

'Good afternoon, sir,' he said, smiling at Scrooge. 'Am I talking to Mr Scrooge or Mr Marley?'

'Marley is dead. He died seven years ago today – on Christmas Eve,' replied Scrooge.

'Mr Scrooge,' said the gentleman, smiling again. 'I have come to ask for your help because it is Christmas. I want money to help the poor people who have no money and no homes.'

'Aren't there any prisons?' asked Scrooge. 'Aren't there any workhouses?'

'Yes, of course there are,' the gentleman replied.

'Good. Good,' said Scrooge. 'I'm pleased. You can put these poor people in prisons and workhouses, can't you?'

'But prisons and workhouses are unpleasant places,' replied the gentleman. 'I am sure you want people to have a merry Christmas. How much money will you give me?'

'None. None at all,' said Scrooge. 'I don't have a merry Christmas. I don't believe in Christmas. I'm not giving money to anyone else so they can have a merry Christmas. Put the poor people in workhouses.'

'Many people fear and hate workhouses. They would rather die than live in workhouses,' replied the gentleman.

'Good,' said Scrooge. 'There are too many people in the world. Tell them to go away and die. Goodbye.'

The gentleman left and Scrooge started working again. Outside it became colder and darker and the fog became thicker. It was so cold that water froze into ice on the streets. But there were bright lights in the windows of the shops. People were buying good things to eat and drink.

In all the shops there was good food for Christmas – fruit and nuts, pies and puddings, turkeys and geese. Everyone bought a turkey or a goose to cook for Christmas dinner.

There was the sound of singing. Boys and girls sang Christmas carols and other people gave them money. A thin boy in torn clothes sang outside Scrooge's window:

We wish you a Merry Christmas.

We wish you a Merry Christmas –

Scrooge shouted angrily and the boy ran away.

At last, Scrooge decided it was time to stop work. Bob Cratchit blew out his candle and put on his hat. He didn't have a coat.

'You want to have a holiday tomorrow, I suppose?' asked Scrooge.

'Yes, please,' replied Bob, 'if it's all right.'

'No, it isn't all right. You will be paid a day's wages and do no work,' said Scrooge.

11

'Christmas Day is only once a year,' said Bob.

'Bah!' said Scrooge. 'I suppose I can't make you work on Christmas Day. Nobody else works. But you must be here very early the next day.'

Bob was happy that it was Christmas. On his way home, he stopped and played with some boys. The boys were sliding down the ice on a steep hill. Bob slid down the ice twenty times! Then he ran home happily to his wife and six children. Scrooge went to an inn to eat his dinner alone.

3

Marley's Ghost

Scrooge finished his dinner and began to walk home. He walked through the streets until he reached his house. His house was big and old. Seven years ago it had belonged to Jacob Marley. Scrooge lived in two of the rooms. The rest of the house was dark and empty.

Scrooge took some heavy keys out of his pocket and unlocked the big wooden front door. There was a metal knocker in the middle of the door. Usually Scrooge did not look at it. But tonight the knocker was different. Scrooge thought he saw something strange. He looked closely and he saw Marley's face in the middle of the knocker!

The old man was very surprised. He opened the door. He looked at the back of it. But the back of Marley's head was not there!

'Bah!' he said, and slammed the door shut.

Scrooge lit a candle and went up the big staircase to his rooms. He unlocked the door and went inside. Then quickly he locked the door again. He put on his night-clothes and sat in a chair close to a very small fire. Then he saw Marley's face again – in the flames of the fire!

Suddenly, a bell above Scrooge's head started to ring. Then another bell! And another! And another! Bells rang all over the empty house. People had once used these bells to call servants to different rooms. But Scrooge lived alone. There were no servants in Scrooge's house.

The bells stopped. Then Scrooge heard another noise. It was a clanking, banging noise and it was getting louder. Someone was pulling metal chains across the floor down-stairs. Now, someone was pulling metal chains up the stairs.

'This isn't happening!' said Scrooge. 'I won't believe it.'

The clanking noise grew louder and louder. Then the noise came straight through the door into Scrooge's room. Suddenly, Scrooge saw Jacob Marley. He saw the face he had seen on the door knocker and in the fire. He saw Marley's face and hair and coat and boots. He saw a white cloth tied round Marley's face and chin. But Scrooge also saw the door. He could see straight through Marley! Was this a ghost?

There were huge chains round Marley's body and on the floor behind him. On the chains were things which Scrooge recognised. There were money-boxes, keys, locks and account books.

'Who are you?' asked Scrooge.

'Ask me who I *was*,' replied the ghost.

'Bah!' said Scrooge. 'Who were you?'

Scrooge could see straight through Marley!
Was this a ghost?

'When I was alive, we worked together. I was your partner, Jacob Marley,' it said.

4

News for Scrooge

'C– Can you sit down?' Scrooge asked the ghost. Scrooge was a little frightened now.

'Yes, I can,' replied the ghost, and it sat down opposite Scrooge.

'You don't believe I'm here, do you?' said the ghost.

Scrooge shook his head. 'No, I don't,' he said.

The ghost shouted loudly and clanked its chains. Then it untied the white cloth and its mouth fell wide open.

Scrooge was very frightened now. He fell onto his knees on the floor in front of Marley's ghost.

'W– W– Why have you come to see me? Why is a dead man here on earth?' Scrooge asked.

'When they are alive, people must go out into the world and help other people,' replied the ghost. 'But some people do not do this. They do not talk to other people or care about them. So, when they die, these people become ghosts. They must travel around the world for ever when they are dead.

'These dead people see terrible things while they are travelling, but they can do nothing to help anyone,' the ghost went on. 'People can only help each other while they are alive.'

The ghost clanked its chains again, making a terrible noise.

Scrooge was still on his knees. His voice shook with fear when he spoke. 'Why are those chains around your body?' he asked.

'I made these chains for myself when I was alive,' said Marley's ghost. 'I was cruel and unkind. So the chains grew longer. I would not give people money. So the chains grew heavier. You, too, have a long and heavy chain.'

Scrooge looked around quickly. He was worried. Was there a chain around his own body? But he could see nothing. Scrooge looked up at the ghost.

'Be kind to me, Jacob,' Scrooge said. 'Give me some comfort.'

'I can give you no comfort. There is no comfort for me,' said the ghost. 'I have been travelling for seven years. I wasn't kind or helpful when I was alive. Now I can do nothing to help anyone. I must travel all the time and see terrible things.'

'But you were a good businessman,' said Scrooge. 'You earned a lot of money.'

The ghost gave a loud cry. 'Oh, no! I was wrong to care about money. Wrong! I wasn't kind to people. I didn't help people.'

Then it spoke again. 'Now, Christmas is the worst time of year for me. Why didn't I help people at Christmas when I was alive?'

Scrooge was very worried. He was like Jacob Marley. He didn't help people. He didn't believe in Christmas. Was he going to be like Marley's ghost when he died?

'I must go soon,' said the ghost suddenly. 'Listen to me. I want to tell you why I am here.'

'Yes, yes, I'll listen to you,' replied Scrooge, 'but be

kind to me, Jacob.'

'I can visit you only once, Ebenezer,' said Marley's ghost. 'I am going to try to help you. Perhaps you will learn to be good and kind. Then you will not travel around the world for ever when you are dead. You will not see terrible things.'

'Thank you, Jacob. You were always a good friend,' said Scrooge.

'Three ghosts will come to see you,' said Marley's ghost.

'Oh no!' said Scrooge in a worried voice. 'Please tell them not to come. I don't want to see them.'

'You cannot be helped if they do not come,' replied Marley's ghost. 'The first ghost will come at one o'clock tomorrow morning. The second ghost will come at one o'clock the next night. The third ghost will come at midnight the following night. You will not see me again.'

The ghost wrapped the white cloth round its face and chin. Then it picked up its chains and walked towards the window.

The window opened slowly as Marley's ghost walked towards it. Scrooge followed the ghost and stopped by the window. Then the ghost walked out of the window and disappeared.

Scrooge looked out of the window. The sky was full of ghosts. Many of them were ghosts of people Scrooge had known. They were all carrying heavy chains and they were crying and shouting.

Scrooge closed the window. Suddenly he felt very tired. It was two o'clock in the morning. He closed the curtains around his bed and lay down. He tried to say 'Humbug!' but he was too tired. He said 'Hum ...' then fell asleep.

17

Scrooge looked out of the window.
The sky was full of ghosts.

5

The Ghost of Christmas Past

When Scrooge woke up, it was very dark. He heard the sound of a bell. There was a clock in the church near Scrooge's house. The bell in the clock rang twelve times. Twelve o'clock! Scrooge was surprised. At two o'clock he had fallen asleep. Now it was twelve o'clock.

'Have I slept for a whole day?' said Scrooge to himself. 'Or is it daytime? Is it midday?' He pulled open the curtains around his bed. 'But it's dark. Is there something wrong with the sun?'

He got out of bed and went to the window. He looked out but he could not see anybody. The city was quiet. Yes, it was twelve o'clock at night.

Scrooge got back into bed and closed the curtains. He was worried and he could not sleep. Then he remembered Marley's ghost. He remembered what the ghost had said. Another ghost was going to visit him at one o'clock in the morning. He lay quietly in his bed. Time passed very slowly.

The bell rang again at a quarter past twelve. Then it rang at half past twelve. Then at a quarter to one. And then it rang once more. It was one o'clock.

Suddenly, a hand pulled back the curtains around the bed. Scrooge looked up and saw the face of another ghost!

The ghost was very strange. It looked like an old man, but it was the same size as a child. Its long hair was white like an old man's hair. But its face was soft and smooth like a child's face. Its arms and hands were big and strong, but its legs and feet were small.

The ghost was wearing a long white robe. It carried a branch from a green holly tree in its hand. Scrooge was not surprised to see the holly. Holly is always green in winter. But he was surprised that the ghost had summer flowers on its robe.

Something else was strange. There was a bright light coming out of the top of the ghost's head. And under its arm it carried a hat – a big, pointed cap.

Then Scrooge saw that the ghost was changing all the time. It had one leg, and then it had twenty legs. It became a body with no head. Then it became a head with no body.

'Marley said a ghost was coming at one o'clock,' said Scrooge. 'Are you the ghost Marley told me about?'

'I am,' replied the ghost quietly.

'Who are you? What are you?' Scrooge asked.

'I am the Ghost of Christmas Past. I am the ghost of your past life.'

'Why have you come?' asked Scrooge.

'I have come to help you,' the ghost replied. It took hold of Scrooge's arm. 'Get out of bed. Come with me.'

The ghost's hand was very strong, but it held Scrooge gently. They went towards the window.

'I'm not a ghost,' said Scrooge. 'I'm a man. I'll fall if I go out of the window.'

'You will not fall,' the ghost said. It held Scrooge's arm.

They went through the window of Scrooge's room. Suddenly they were standing in the middle of a road. The city had gone and there were fields next to the road. It was a cold winter's day and there was snow on the ground.

'I know where we are!' said Scrooge. 'I lived near here when I was a boy.'

The ghost was wearing a long white robe. It carried a branch from a green holly tree in its hand.

6
Scrooge as a Boy

Scrooge looked at the fields all around him.

'Yes,' he said. 'I lived near here when I was a boy.'

Scrooge suddenly felt very happy. Then he felt afraid. Then he felt happy again. Then he felt sad.

'Is that a tear in your eye?' said the ghost very quietly. 'Are you crying?'

'No, no,' said Scrooge quickly.

Scrooge and the ghost walked along the road until they saw a small town. Scrooge recognised the town. He knew the church and the river and the bridge.

Then he saw some boys riding horses. They came towards him and Scrooge recognised all the boys too. He remembered their names. The boys were very happy. They were shouting to each other. 'Merry Christmas! Merry Christmas!'

'They cannot see you,' said the ghost. 'They are people from your past life.'

Scrooge was happy when he heard the boys shout 'Merry Christmas!'

'Why am I happy?' he asked himself. 'I don't like Christmas. It's nonsense. It's humbug.'

'There is a school near here,' said the ghost. 'There is one child in the school. His friends have forgotten him. He is lonely.'

'I know,' replied Scrooge. 'I remember.'

The ghost and Scrooge walked towards the school. It was an old brick building. They went into a long, cold room. There was a sad little boy sitting beside a small fire.

Scrooge sat down next to the boy. There were tears on Scrooge's face.

'Poor boy,' he said. 'I wish — '

'What do you wish?' asked the ghost.

'It's too late now,' replied Scrooge. 'Last night a boy stood outside my office. He sang a Christmas carol. I told him to go away. Now, I wish I could give him some money.'

The ghost smiled. 'I am going to show you another Christmas in this school,' it said.

The room changed. It became darker and dirtier and older. The boy grew bigger and older. He was still lonely and sad.

Suddenly the door opened. Scrooge saw a young girl run into the room. She ran to the boy. She put her arms round the boy's neck and kissed him.

'I've come to take you home, Ebenezer,' she shouted happily.

'Home, Frances?' said the boy. 'Can I come home?'

'Yes,' she replied. 'Father says you can come home now. You don't have to come back to school again. Father sent me to take you home.

'You're coming home for Christmas. The carriage is waiting outside.'

Soon Scrooge saw the children get into the carriage. He saw the horses pull the carriage away from the school.

'Your sister, Frances, was a kind girl,' the ghost said. 'And she was kind when she was a woman too. She died a long time ago, but she had a child, didn't she?'

'Yes,' said Scrooge. 'She had a son.'

'Your nephew, Fred,' said the ghost.

'Yes,' replied Scrooge.

Then suddenly Scrooge and the ghost were in a city.

'I've come to take you home, Ebenezer,' the young girl
shouted happily.

The streets were full of people and carriages and horses. It was dark and cold. But there were bright lights in the shops. People were buying good things to eat and drink. It was a different Christmas from Scrooge's past life.

7

Christmas with the Fezziwigs

Scrooge and the Ghost of Christmas Past walked through the busy streets of the city. The ghost stopped outside the door of a big building.

'Do you remember this place?' it asked.

'Yes, of course I remember,' replied Scrooge. 'I worked here after I left school.'

They went into the building and saw an old gentleman sitting in an office. He was sitting on a very high chair and he was writing numbers in a big account book.

'It's old Fezziwig!' shouted Scrooge. 'Dear old Fezziwig!'

As Scrooge spoke, the old gentleman put down his pen. He looked at a clock. It was seven o'clock. Fezziwig smiled, then he laughed. He clapped his hands together. He was a very happy old man.

'Ebenezer! Dick!' shouted Fezziwig.

Two young men ran into the office. And Scrooge saw himself as a young man.

'Look,' said Scrooge to the ghost. 'There's Dick Wilkins with me. He liked me. He was a good friend.'

'No more work tonight, boys,' said Fezziwig. 'It's Christmas Eve.'

Fezziwig clapped his hands again and jumped down

from his high chair.

'Move the desks, boys,' he said. 'Move the chairs. Put lots of coal on the fire. Make the room bright and merry!'

Soon a man arrived. He was carrying a violin. Mrs Fezziwig arrived. She was smiling and happy like her husband. Then Mr and Mrs Fezziwig's three daughters arrived. They were smiling and happy too. Then six young men who were in love with the daughters came in. And the Fezziwigs' servants and a young man who lived across the road arrived. The musician started to play his violin and the party began.

The young people danced. They played games and they ate lots of food. Old Mr and Mrs Fezziwig danced and laughed!

At eleven o'clock the party finished. Mr and Mrs Fezziwig stood by the door. They shook hands with everyone as they left. 'Merry Christmas!' they all said. 'Merry Christmas!'

At last, everyone had gone except Ebenezer and Dick. They lived with Mr and Mrs Fezziwig. The two old people shook hands with them. Then Ebenezer and Dick went to bed. They both slept in beds in the office.

While he watched the party, old Scrooge had forgotten about the ghost. Suddenly he saw that the ghost was looking at him again. The light coming out of its head was very bright.

'It is very easy to make people happy, isn't it?' the ghost said. 'Listen.'

Scrooge listened to Dick and Ebenezer talking.

'Mr and Mrs Fezziwig are dear, kind people. They are so good to us,' said the young men.

'Fezziwig did not spend much money,' the ghost went on.

The young people danced. They played games and ate lots of
food. Old Mr and Mrs Fezziwig danced and laughed!

'So why did people like him so much?'

'The money was not important,' replied Scrooge. 'We worked for him and he was able make us happy or unhappy. He was able make our work hard or easy. The happiness he gave us was important, not the money he spent.'

The Ghost of Christmas Past looked carefully at Scrooge and Scrooge suddenly stopped talking.

'What are you thinking about?' asked the ghost.

'Oh, nothing much,' replied Scrooge. 'I was ... I was wishing I could speak a few words to Bob Cratchit.'

The ghost did not speak for a few moments. Then it said, 'I do not have much time left.'

8

The Girl Who Loved Scrooge

Mr and Mrs Fezziwig disappeared. So did Dick and the young Ebenezer.

Then Scrooge saw himself again, but now he was a few years older. He looked serious and worried. Scrooge was looking at himself in his past life again.

There was a beautiful young girl sitting next to Ebenezer. She was wearing a black dress and she was crying.

It was Christmas once again, but it was not a happy Christmas.

'A few years ago we got engaged, Ebenezer,' said the girl. 'We decided to get married when we had enough money. But you have changed. Now you care more about money than you care about me. You do not have to marry me. We can break our engagement.'

'Belle, I have never asked to break our engagement,' replied Ebenezer.

'No,' she said. 'But it's true, isn't it? You love money more than you love me.'

'Yes,' he replied quietly. The girl stood up and walked away from him. She left him for ever.

'Oh, Ghost of Christmas Past!' cried Scrooge. 'Take me home. I don't want to see any more.'

'There is one more place you must see,' said the ghost, and it held Scrooge with a strong hand. 'Look over there!'

Scrooge saw a warm, comfortable room. The room was full of noisy, happy children. A beautiful young girl was sitting by the fire.

At first, Scrooge thought it was Belle. But then he saw Belle sitting opposite the girl. Belle was many years older now, but she was still beautiful. The girl was Belle's daughter.

The door opened and a man came in, He was carrying toys and Christmas presents. The children ran to meet their father who laughed and played with them. At last, the man sat down with his wife and eldest daughter.

Scrooge watched sadly. Why wasn't this woman his wife? Why wasn't this girl his daughter?

'Belle,' said the man to his wife. 'I saw someone you used to know today. Who do you think it was?'

The woman laughed. 'Was it Mr Scrooge?'

'Yes, it was. I walked past his office. He was sitting there on his own. His partner, Jacob Marley, died today. So now Scrooge is alone. He has no friends and no family.'

'Ghost of Christmas Past,' said Scrooge, 'please, please

Scrooge watched sadly. Why wasn't this woman his wife?
Why wasn't this girl his daughter?

take me away from this place. I don't want to see any more.'

'These things all happened in your past life,' said the ghost to the old man. 'You made them happen.'

'Please,' said Scrooge, 'please let me go home.'

When he looked at the ghost's face, Scrooge saw lots of different faces. He saw the faces of all the people from his past life. The bright light shone out of the top of the ghost's head.

Quickly, Scrooge took hold of the pointed cap that was under the ghost's arm. He put the cap on the ghost's head. He pushed the cap down as hard as he could. But the light did not go out. It shone down onto the ground.

Scrooge was very tired. Suddenly he was back in his own room. He lay down on his bed and immediately fell asleep.

9

The Ghost of Christmas Present

When Scrooge woke up again, it was dark. He knew that the next ghost was going to arrive soon.

What would this ghost look like? Scrooge was ready for the next ghost. He did not care if it looked like a baby or an elephant!

The church bell rang once. It was one o'clock. Scrooge pulled back the curtains around his bed and waited. There was a bright, red-coloured light around his bed, but there was no ghost.

Five minutes passed. Ten minutes. Fifteen minutes. Scrooge lay in his bed, very frightened. At last, he saw that the strange light was coming from under the door of the next room. He got out of bed and walked slowly towards the door.

A voice suddenly called his name. 'Come in, Ebenezer Scrooge. Come in.'

Scrooge opened the door and looked into the room. Yes, it was his room. But it had changed! It looked completely different.

There were branches of trees hanging everywhere. All the branches were covered with bright green leaves and little red berries. There was a huge fire with lots of bright yellow flames. It was the biggest fire Scrooge had ever seen in that room. And there was food! Lots and lots of food! There were turkeys and geese. There was fruit. There were pies and puddings. There were all the good things that people eat at Christmas.

In the middle of the room was a huge, smiling man. He was holding a big torch. The torch looked like an animal's horn. A small, bright, red flame was burning at the top of it. This was the light that Scrooge had seen.

'Come in,' shouted the huge man. He had a kind voice and a kind face. But Scrooge did not want to look at him.

'I am the Ghost of Christmas Present,' the huge man said to Scrooge. 'Look at me.'

Scrooge saw that the ghost was wearing a long green and white robe. The ghost's hair was long and brown. There were leaves from a holly tree around the top of his head. There was ice on the holly leaves.

'Have you ever seen anyone like me before?' asked the ghost.

'No. Never,' replied Scrooge.

The ghost stood up. 'Take me with you,' said Scrooge.

In the middle of the room was a huge, smiling man. He was holding a big torch.

'Last night I saw many things that happened in my past life. I learnt many things. Tonight I want to go out and learn more. I want to learn to live a better life.'

'Take hold of my robe,' said the Ghost of Christmas Present.

Scrooge took hold of the green and white robe and the room disappeared. Suddenly it was morning and they were standing in a London street. There was snow on the ground and there were lots of people everywhere. It was a sunny, cold Christmas morning. Church bells were ringing and people were coming out of the churches. They were going home to eat their Christmas dinners.

Other people were carrying baskets along the streets. There were geese and turkeys in the baskets. These poor people couldn't cook their Christmas dinners at home because they didn't have ovens. They were taking their Christmas turkeys or geese to the baker's shops. Bakers didn't bake bread on Christmas Day. On Christmas Day, they cooked poor people's Christmas dinners in their big ovens.

Most of these people were happy. When the Ghost of Christmas Present saw people who were sad or angry, he stopped. He waved his torch over their heads. The light from its red flame shone on them. Then these people smiled and laughed happily too.

Scrooge was pleased. The ghost wanted to make the poor people happy.

10
Christmas with the Cratchits

The church bells stopped ringing. Scrooge took hold of the ghost's robe again and they continued their journey. No one could see them as they went through the streets of the city.

They went past many small houses and at last they stopped. The Ghost of Christmas Present had found Bob Cratchit's house. It was a small house with two rooms downstairs and two rooms upstairs. Bob Cratchit, his wife and six children lived in this small house.

The ghost waved the torch and the light from its red flame shone on the little house. Scrooge was pleased that the ghost cared about Bob Cratchit and his family.

Then suddenly Scrooge and the ghost were inside the house. Mrs Cratchit and one of her daughters, Belinda, were putting plates and knives and forks on a table. They were getting ready to eat their Christmas dinner. A boy, Peter, and two smaller children were there too. They were very excited.

'Where's Martha?' asked Mrs Cratchit. 'I hope she won't be late.'

'I'm here, Mother,' said her eldest daughter, coming in the door. 'I'm late because I had a lot of work to do today.'

The little children were looking out of the window. 'Here's Father! Here's Father coming home from church!' they cried. 'Let's play a joke on Father. Hide, Martha! Hide behind the door.'

So quickly Martha hid behind the door, as Bob came

in. Bob was carrying Tiny Tim, his youngest child. Carefully, Bob lifted his son off his shoulders and put him on the floor. The little boy could not walk properly. He had metal bands around his legs to help him to walk. He also leant on a wooden crutch.

'Where's Martha?' asked Bob.

'She's at work. She can't come,' replied his wife.

'Can't come?' said Bob. Suddenly he looked very sad.

Martha did not want to make her father unhappy. 'Oh, Father, I'm here!' she cried. She ran out from behind the door and put her arms round her father. 'It was a joke! Don't be sad.'

'Come and see the Christmas pudding, Tiny Tim,' said Peter. 'It's cooking in a big pot over the fire.'

The younger children took their little brother to the other room to see the special Christmas fruit pudding.

'Did Tiny Tim behave himself well in church?' asked Mrs Cratchit.

'He behaved himself very well,' replied Bob. 'He's always a good child. He always cares about other people, and not about himself.'

The children came back into the room. Tiny Tim sat on his little chair by the fire. Mrs Cratchit spoke to Peter and the two younger children.

'The goose will be cooked now,' she said. 'Go to the baker's shop and bring it back for me.'

And so, Scrooge and the Ghost of Christmas Present watched the Cratchits eat their Christmas dinner. There were eight people and the goose was small. They all said how good the goose tasted. They talked about how little money the goose had cost. But nobody said how small it was!

Martha ran out from behind the door and put her arms round her father.

Then Mrs Cratchit brought in the Christmas pudding. There were eight people and the pudding was small. Everyone said how good it tasted. But nobody said how small it was.

After dinner, Bob poured a drink into everyone's cup. Then he lifted his cup and said, 'A Merry Christmas to us all, my dears! God bless us!'

All the Cratchits lifted their cups too. And Tiny Tim said, 'God bless all of us!'

Bob held his youngest child's hand. Tiny Tim was his favourite child. Tiny Tim was weak and ill. But Bob had no money to pay a doctor. Bob was worried that Tiny Tim would die soon.

Scrooge was looking at Bob Cratchit and Tiny Tim. 'Ghost,' he said suddenly, 'tell me that Tiny Tim will live. Tell me that the little boy won't die.'

'This family is very poor,' replied the ghost. 'They cannot buy enough food. They cannot pay a doctor. The little boy will die if the family does not get medicine and more food. There will be an empty chair beside the fire. There will be a wooden crutch that nobody uses.'

'Oh, no,' said Scrooge.

'Yes, the little boy will die,' repeated the ghost.

Then it said, 'There are too many people in the world. Tell them to go away and die.'

Scrooge looked at the ghost in horror. Those were his own words. He remembered the gentleman who had come to his office. The gentleman had asked for money to help the poor people in London.

Then Scrooge heard Bob Cratchit speaking again. Bob was lifting his cup once more. 'And God bless Mr Scrooge,' he said.

'Oh no, Bob,' said Mrs Cratchit. 'Mr Scrooge doesn't care about you. He doesn't care about us. He only cares about money.'

'It's Christmas Day,' replied Bob. 'We must all drink and give our good wishes to Mr Scrooge.'

So all the family drank and said, 'God bless Mr Scrooge.'

Soon all the Cratchits were happy again. They talked and laughed and sang songs. Tiny Tim sang in a sweet but quiet voice:

The snow was cold!

The child was lost!

His home was far away ...

The light from the ghost's torch shone down on the Cratchit family and they were all happy.

11

A Merry Christmas Everywhere

Soon Scrooge and the Ghost of Christmas Present left the Cratchits' house and moved on through the streets. It was starting to get dark.

Happy people were going to visit friends and relations to wish them a merry Christmas. The ghost waved his torch over them all and laughed loudly.

Suddenly, the city disappeared and everything changed. Scrooge saw grass and rocks below him, and lakes that were covered in ice.

The sun was going down and soon it was dark and very

cold.

'Where are we?' asked Scrooge.

'We are in a place where miners live,' replied the ghost. 'They dig for coal under the ground. They are poor people, but they know about me. Look!'

Scrooge saw a big family in a very small stone house. Old people and young people were sitting together around a fire and they were singing a Christmas song.

'Take hold of my robe again,' said the ghost. Then the journey continued. Sometimes it was day and sometimes it was night. Scrooge saw that the ghost was getting older. Its hair was grey now.

Scrooge was frightened when they flew out over the sea. He saw a lighthouse on some dangerous rocks. The bright light from the lighthouse told ships to keep away from the rocks. The two men who lived in the lighthouse were far away from their homes and their families. But

they were laughing and saying 'Merry Christmas' to each other.

The ghost took Scrooge farther out to sea. There Scrooge saw a ship. The sailors on the ship were talking about their families. They sang Christmas songs and they were happy.

Then Scrooge suddenly heard somebody laugh. He had heard that laugh before. It was the laugh of his nephew, Fred.

Now Scrooge and the ghost were in Fred's bright, clean house. It was full of people. There was Fred, and his wife, who was very pretty. There were his wife's sisters and there was a friend called Mr Topper.

As before, no one could see Scrooge or the ghost. Fred was talking and laughing. Scrooge listened. Fred was talking about his uncle – about him!

'Uncle Scrooge said Christmas is nonsense. He said, "It's humbug! Bah!"' said Fred. The young man was laughing, but he was being kind too.

'Your uncle is a miserable old man,' said Fred's wife. 'He doesn't care about anybody. He only cares about his money.'

'He's a strange old man. His money doesn't make him happy,' replied Fred. 'I feel sorry for him. I asked him to come and have Christmas dinner with us today. He wouldn't come. But I can't be angry with him. He makes himself unhappy.

'I'm going to say "Merry Christmas" to Uncle Scrooge every year,' Fred went on. 'I'm going to ask him to come to dinner every year at Christmas.'

Everybody laughed again, then they started to play games. Scrooge enjoyed watching all the games. He wanted to play them too.

The ghost smiled at Scrooge. He was pleased that the old man was enjoying Fred's Christmas party.

'Can we stay here, please?' Scrooge asked the ghost. He sounded like an excited child. 'Can we stay here for a long time?'

Scrooge watched another game.

'I am thinking of a person,' said Fred to his wife and friends. 'You must guess who this person is. Ask me questions. I will answer Yes or No.'

They asked questions. They tried to guess who Fred was thinking about. Fred was thinking of a person who was like an unpleasant animal. This animal made unfriendly noises.

'I know! I know!' said one of the sisters. 'It's your Uncle Scrooge!'

They all laughed.

'Now we must all drink and wish "Merry Christmas" to my uncle,' said Scrooge's nephew. 'We have laughed at him tonight, so we must be kind to him too.'

Fred lifted a glass of wine. 'Merry Christmas, Uncle, wherever you are,' he said.

Scrooge wished he could say 'Thank you' to his nephew. But he could not think about Fred any more. The ghost took Scrooge away to more houses and more parties. Everywhere, the ghost waved the torch and made people happy.

Days and nights passed. The ghost became older and older as they travelled. Scrooge saw that the ghost's hair was now white.

'Do you have to go soon?' asked Scrooge.

'Yes. I do not have much time left,' said the Ghost of

The ghost smiled at Scrooge. He was pleased that the old man was enjoying Fred's Christmas party.

Christmas Present. 'I must go tonight at midnight.'

They were in a London street. Scrooge heard church bells ring. It was a quarter to midnight.

Then he saw a small, child's hand. It was holding the ghost's robe.

'Who's this?' asked Scrooge.

The ghost pulled two children from behind him. There was a boy and a girl. They were thin children, wearing torn clothes. They looked frightened, angry and hungry. They did not look friendly.

Scrooge was surprised. 'Ghost, are these your children?' he asked.

'No,' said the ghost. 'These are poor children from the streets of London.'

Scrooge was very sad. 'Poor children!' he said. 'Don't they have homes? Children need homes.'

'Aren't there any prisons? Aren't there any workhouses? Put the poor people in workhouses,' said the ghost.

Scrooge remembered those words. They were his own words. He had said them to the gentleman who came to his office. The gentleman had asked him for money to help the poor people.

The church bells rang twelve times. It was midnight. Scrooge opened his mouth to speak to the ghost. But the huge man in the green and white robe had gone.

Then Scrooge saw something coming towards him. It was another ghost. This ghost wore a long black robe which touched the ground. Its head and face were covered by a large hood.

Scrooge remembered the words of Marley's ghost. 'The third ghost will come at midnight ...'

12

The Ghost of Christmas Yet to Come

The third ghost came towards Scrooge slowly and quietly. It wore a long black robe which hid its body and its face. The ghost was pointing at Scrooge. It did not speak to him.

Scrooge *had* been a little afraid of the first two ghosts. But the Ghost of Christmas Past and the Ghost of Christmas Present had been friendly. They had spoken to him. But now Scrooge was very frightened. He fell onto his knees on the ground in front of the ghost.

'Are you the Ghost of Christmas Yet to Come?' Scrooge asked.

The terrible ghost did not answer. Now its hand was pointing past Scrooge. The ghost was showing Scrooge where they were going to go.

'Ghost of the future, I am afraid of you,' said Scrooge. 'I want to be a better man. I will come with you. Thank you for coming to help me. But please talk to me.'

The ghost's hand continued to point past Scrooge. The ghost did not speak.

Very frightened, Scrooge stood up. He took hold of the ghost's black robe. Immediately, they were in another part of London.

There were men everywhere. They were walking around very quickly. They were talking and looking at their watches. They were carrying account books like Scrooge's account books.

Scrooge knew where he was. He was in the Exchange.

This was the place where businessmen came to talk. They came here to buy and sell things. This was the place where Scrooge came to do his business every day.

The ghost stopped next to a group of men. Scrooge recognised them. The ghost pointed at them. It was telling Scrooge to listen to their conversation.

Scrooge knew the men could not see him. So he stood near them and listened to them.

'When did he die?' asked one of the men.

'Last night,' replied another man.

'Who will go to his funeral?' asked a third man.

'I don't know. Will anybody go to his funeral?' replied the second man. 'He didn't have any friends.'

Scrooge looked at the ghost. 'Who are they talking about?' he asked.

The ghost did not reply. It pointed at two more men. Scrooge knew these men too. They were very important businessmen.

'I've heard that he's dead,' said one of them.

'Yes, he is,' replied the other. 'It's cold today, isn't it?'

Scrooge was surprised. Someone had died. Nobody cared about the person who had died. Who were these people talking about? Why was the ghost telling him to listen to their conversations?

Then the ghost moved on. Soon they were in another part of London. This was a dirty, old part of the city where poor people lived. The ghost took Scrooge into a dirty little shop. Inside the shop there were old cooking pots, broken furniture and piles of dirty, torn clothes. An old man with grey hair sat in a corner smoking a pipe.

A woman came into the shop carrying a large bundle of cloth. An older woman came in carrying a smaller bundle of cloth. Then a man wearing a black suit came in. They all looked at each other in surprise.

Old Joe, the owner of the shop, locked the door. He took his visitors into a room behind the shop.

The women put down their bundles. 'It isn't wrong to take a few things from a dead man,' the older woman said.

'That's true. He's dead now. He doesn't need them,' said the other woman. 'We must look after ourselves.'

The three visitors all had things to sell to Old Joe. The man in the black suit did not have many things. He took

a watch and a few silver buttons out of his pocket.

The older woman had a few clothes and some bed sheets in her bundle. Old Joe did not pay them very much money.

But the woman with the large bundle had stolen the curtains from around a dead man's bed. She had also stolen the wool blankets from his bed. And she had stolen the clothes from the body of the dead man.

'He had no friends,' the woman said. 'No relatives came to the house when he died. So we took the things we wanted.'

Scrooge listened in horror to their conversation. 'I understand why you have brought me here,' he said to the ghost. 'I must learn to care about people. People will steal from me when I die if I do not learn to care.'

The shop disappeared. Scrooge was now in a dark, cold room. There was a bed without curtains around it. On the bed was something covered by a thin sheet. Scrooge was frightened. He knew there was a body under the sheet. This was the body of the man who had no friends.

The ghost pointed at the body under the sheet. 'No, I can't,' said Scrooge. 'I can't lift up the sheet. I can't look at him. I understand why you are showing me this man. Please let us leave this place now!'

The ghost did not move. 'Please,' said Scrooge, 'show me somebody who cares about this man's death. Please!'
The ghost lifted its arms high in the air. The long black robe hung down to the ground in front of Scrooge. When the ghost lowered its arms again, Scrooge saw a room behind it.

There was a young woman in the room with her two children. She was worried and she was walking round and

'No, I can't,' said Scrooge. 'I can't lift up the sheet.'

round the room.

The door opened and the woman's husband came in.

'Is there any news?' asked the woman quickly. 'Is there good news or bad news?'

'There is good news for us,' replied the young man. 'I went to the old man's house. I was going to tell him that we can't pay him. I went to say that we'll pay him next week. But he's dead, Caroline. The old man is dead.'

'It's wrong to be happy because someone is dead,' said the woman. 'But I am happy.

'Who must we pay now?' she went on.

'I don't know,' replied her husband. 'But someone else will be kinder to us than that old man. I'm happy too.'

Scrooge was horrified. This man and woman cared. But they were happy because the man had died!

'Ghost of Christmas Yet to Come,' he said, 'please take me somewhere else. Show me someone else who has died. But show me people who are sad about the death.'

13

Tiny Tim

The ghost did not speak and Scrooge took hold of the black robe. They moved on again. They moved through streets which Scrooge recognised. But he could not see himself anywhere. He had seen himself in his past life as a child and as a young man. But he could not see himself in the future.

The ghost stopped in front of a house which Scrooge recognised. It was Bob Cratchit's house.

Scrooge saw Mrs Cratchit and the children inside the house. They were all very quiet. Mrs Cratchit and her daughters were sewing. They were making black clothes. So Scrooge knew that someone had died. Peter was reading the Bible aloud. He was reading a story about Jesus and a little child, and he was crying.

Peter stopped reading. 'Father is late again tonight,' he said.

All the children looked sad.

'Father walked home quickly when Tiny Tim was alive,' said Mrs Cratchit quietly. 'He loved to carry Tiny Tim on his shoulders.'

When Bob arrived home, the children all ran to meet him at the door.

Bob looked at the black clothes. 'Have you finished making them?' he asked. 'Will our clothes be ready to wear at the funeral on Sunday? I have been to the church today. I have made arrangements for Tiny Tim's funeral.'

Then he sat down and cried.

At last, Bob went upstairs. Tiny Tim's body was lying on a bed. Bob sat next to the bed and he looked at his dead son. Then he smiled. He kissed Tiny Tim's little face and he went downstairs again.

The Cratchit family sat next to the fire and talked. 'Mr Scrooge's nephew spoke very kindly to me. He was sad to hear about Tiny Tim,' said Bob. 'He said he will help us. He will give Peter a job.'

'Yes, Peter is nearly twelve now. He must have a job,' said Mrs Cratchit. 'The children will all need jobs soon.'

'We must always remember Tiny Tim,' said Bob. 'He was a good child and a happy child. Promise me that you will always remember him.'

They all promised.

Scrooge watched the sad family. Then he spoke to the ghost. 'I think that you will soon leave me,' he said. 'You have shown me many things. But please tell me, who was the man who died?'

The Ghost of Christmas Yet to Come pointed past Scrooge and they moved on again. They went back to the part of London that Scrooge knew well. They passed the building which had 'Scrooge and Marley' written above the door.

'Stop, Ghost,' said Scrooge.

But the ghost kept on moving. Scrooge ran back to look through the window into his office. The room was the same, but there was different furniture. And the man sitting in the room was not Scrooge!

Scrooge ran back to the ghost. Soon they arrived at a church.

The ghost went through the gates into the churchyard. It moved past many gravestones. Then it stopped and pointed down at a grave.

Scrooge was frightened, very frightened. At last, he looked at the name on the gravestone: EBENEZER SCROOGE.

'No, Ghost! Oh, no, no!' he cried. But the ghost pointed at Scrooge, then pointed at the ground.

'Listen to me,' cried Scrooge, taking hold of the ghost's black robe. 'You have shown me many terrible things. Are they all going to happen? Can I stop them from happening?'

Scrooge fell onto his knees in front of the ghost. 'You are a good ghost, aren't you? You are here to help me, aren't you? All three of you came to help me.

At last, Scrooge looked at the name on the gravestone.

'I will live a better life. I will care about people. I will care about Christmas. I will think about the Past, the Present and the Future. Please tell me that these things will not happen.'

Scrooge tried to hold the ghost's robe. But suddenly he was back in his bedroom. He was holding one of the wooden posts at the end of his bed.

14

A Changed Man

Scrooge closed his eyes, then opened them again. Yes, he was in his own bedroom. And he was alive!

'God bless you, Jacob Marley,' he said. 'Thank you for coming to help me. Thank you for sending the three ghosts.'

Scrooge was happy. He was very, very happy. He ran round his room. He got dressed very quickly.

'I'm very happy!' he cried. 'I'm happy! Happy! Happy! Merry Christmas to everybody! Happy Christmas to everybody in the world!'

Scrooge ran into the other room. He looked at the door where Marley's ghost had come in. He looked at the window where the ghost had gone out. He looked at the places where the other ghosts had been.

Scrooge knew that he had met the ghosts. He knew that all those things had happened. And Scrooge laughed. Scrooge had not laughed for many years and now he laughed very loudly.

'What day is it?' he said suddenly. 'How long have I

been away?'

Then church bells started to ring. All the church bells in London started to ring. Scrooge ran to the window and opened it.

'What day is it?' he shouted down to a boy in the street.

The boy looked very surprised. Then he replied. 'It's Christmas Day, of course!'

'Christmas Day!' shouted Scrooge. 'I haven't missed it. All those things happened in one night.

'Boy!' he shouted. 'Do you know the shop at the end of the street? Do you know the shop with a huge turkey hanging in its window?'

'Do you mean the turkey that's as big as me?' asked the boy.

'Yes, yes,' said Scrooge. 'I want you to go and buy it for me. Tell the man in the shop to bring the turkey here. Here's some money for you!' And Scrooge threw some coins down.

Scrooge went downstairs. He waited for the man to bring the turkey. He looked at the door knocker. He remembered seeing Marley's face there.

'I shall always love this door knocker,' he said to himself.

The man arrived with the huge turkey. 'I want you to take the turkey to this address,' Scrooge said to him. And he told the man where Bob Cratchit lived.

Then Scrooge went out for a walk. He met the gentleman who had asked him for money.

'I'm very sorry I did not help you yesterday,' said Scrooge. Then he whispered in the man's ear.

The man looked very surprised. 'That's a lot of money.

Do you want to give that much money?' he asked.

'Oh, yes! Yes!' replied Scrooge. 'I want to give you a lot of money!'

Scrooge walked on. He talked to the children he met in the streets. He talked to the poor people. At last, he arrived at a house and knocked on the door. His nephew opened it.

'Hello, Fred,' said Scrooge. 'Can I come in?'

Fred smiled and shook his uncle's hand. 'You're very welcome, Uncle,' he replied.

Scrooge and the Ghost of Christmas Present had watched Fred's wonderful party. Now Scrooge had come to the party. He ate good food and drank good wine. He laughed and played games with Fred, and Fred's pretty wife, and all their happy friends.

Next morning Scrooge arrived early at his office. He was hoping that Bob Cratchit would be late for work. And Bob was late. He did not arrive at nine o'clock. He did not arrive at quarter past nine. It was eighteen and a half minutes past nine when Bob arrived.

'You are very late!' Scrooge said to Bob. 'Come into my room.'

Bob was very worried. Was he going to lose his job? 'Christmas Day is only once a year,' he said.

'Yes, that's right,' said Scrooge. 'There's only one Christmas Day in a year.' Scrooge put his hand on Bob's shoulder. 'So I am going to pay you more. I'm going to raise your wages!'

Bob was very surprised. Was Scrooge mad?

Then Scrooge said, 'Merry Christmas, Bob!' The old man spoke kindly. So Bob knew that Scrooge was not mad.

'Thank you, sir,' Bob said.

'I am going to pay you more. I'm going to raise your wages!'
said Scrooge.

'Merry Christmas, Bob,' Scrooge repeated. 'Now, we must talk about your family. Your boy, Peter, will need a job soon. And we must look after Tiny Tim, mustn't we? This afternoon we'll talk about how I can help.

'But first,' Scrooge went on, 'here's some money. Please go out and buy some more coal!'

———

Scrooge did help Bob and his family. Tiny Tim did not die. Scrooge cared for the little boy and loved him always.

Scrooge made many friends. He laughed and he smiled. He talked to everybody. He spent his money and helped the poor people. Some people laughed at the old man because he had changed so much. But Scrooge did not care.

Scrooge did not ever meet another ghost. But he enjoyed Christmas more than anyone else in the world!

Points for Understanding

1

1 When does this story begin?
2 Two names are painted on the door of an old building. One name is Scrooge. What is the other name?
3 Describe Ebenezer Scrooge.
4 What does Scrooge like? What doesn't he like?

2

1 Why is Bob Cratchit cold?
2 Who is the first visitor to Scrooge's office? Why has he come?
3 Why isn't Scrooge happy to see him?
4 Who is the second visitor to Scrooge's office?
5 Why won't Scrooge help this visitor?
6 Why is there lots of food in the shops?
7 What are people singing in the streets?

3

1 Why does Scrooge look closely at the metal knocker on his big front door?
2 What does Scrooge see when he sits by the fire?
3 Bells ring all over the house. Then they stop ringing. What happens next?
4 Who is Scrooge's visitor? Describe this visitor.

4

1 'Why are those chains around your body?' Scrooge asks Marley's ghost.
What does the ghost reply?
2 Why has the ghost come to see Scrooge?
3 What is going to happen to Scrooge now?

4 What does Scrooge see out of the window?

5

1 What happens at one o'clock in the morning?
2 Who has come to see Scrooge?
3 What does this visitor look like?
4 What is this visitor called?

6

1 'They cannot see you,' said the ghost. 'They are people from your past life.'
   Where has the ghost of Christmas Past taken Scrooge? Who can Scrooge see? How does Scrooge feel?
2 Who is the small boy sitting in the old school building?
3 The ghost shows Scrooge the school at another time. Scrooge sees a boy and a young girl. Who are they?
4 What happened to the young girl when she grew up?

7

1 Scrooge and the Ghost of Christmas Past see an old gentleman sitting in an office. Who is the gentleman?
2 Who comes into the office when the gentleman calls out?
3 What happens next?
4 'Why do people like him so much?' asked the ghost.
   Who is the ghost talking about? What does Scrooge reply?

8

1 Who is the beautiful girl in the black dress? Who is she talking to?
2 What are the two young people talking about?
3 Who do the Ghost of Christmas Past and Scrooge see next? These people talk about Scrooge. What do they say? How does Scrooge feel about this?

9

1 Where does Scrooge find the Ghost of Christmas Present?

2 What does the ghost look like?
3 The ghost takes Scrooge out into the streets of London.
  What does Scrooge see?
4 What does the Ghost carry in his hand? What does he do
  with this thing?

10

1 Bob Cratchit lives in a very small house. How many other
  people live there?
2 Martha hides behind the door. Who comes in through the
  door?
3 Why do Peter and the two younger children go to the
  baker's?
4 Bob Cratchit is worried about Tiny Tim. Why?
5 The ghost tells Scrooge about Tiny Tim. What is going to
  happen to the boy?

11

1 The Ghost of Christmas Present takes Scrooge to many
  different places. Where do they go?
2 Who do Scrooge and the ghost see in Fred's house?
3 'I'm going to say "Merry Christmas" to Uncle Scrooge every
  year.'
  Who said this? Why did he say it?
4 'Put the poor people in workhouses,' said the ghost.
  Why does the ghost say this? Why does Scrooge remember
  these words?
5 The church bells ring at midnight. The ghost in the green
  and white robe disappears. What happens next?

12

1 Why is Scrooge very frightened by the third ghost?
2 What is the name of the third ghost?
3 Scrooge hears some businessmen talking. What are they
  talking about?
4 Three people come to a dirty little shop. Why have they
  come?

5 Scrooge sees a bed in a cold, dark room. Why is he frightened?

13

1 Scrooge says, 'Show me someone else who has died. But show me people who are sad about the death.'
Where does the Ghost of Christmas Yet to Come take him?
2 Who is dead?
3 The ghost takes Scrooge to the churchyard. What do they see there?
4 What promises does Scrooge make?

14

1 How does Scrooge feel when he wakes up?
2 What day is it?
3 Scrooge gives a young boy some money. He tells him to buy a huge turkey. Who does Scrooge give the turkey to?
4 Who does Scrooge give money to?
5 Who does Scrooge go to visit?
6 Is Scrooge angry when Bob Cratchit is late for work? What does Scrooge say that he will do?
7 How has Scrooge changed since the beginning of the story?

A Christmas Carol *by Charles Dickens*
Riders of the Purple Sage *by Zane Grey*
The Canterville Ghost and Other Stories *by Oscar Wilde*
Lady Portia's Revenge and Other Stories *by David Evans*
The Picture of Dorian Gray *by Oscar Wilde*
Treasure Island *by Robert Louis Stevenson*
Road to Nowhere *by John Milne*
The Black Cat *by John Milne*
Don't Tell Me What To Do *by Michael Hardcastle*
The Runaways *by Victor Canning*
The Red Pony *by John Steinbeck*
The Goalkeeper's Revenge and Other Stories *by Bill Naughton*
The Stranger *by Norman Whitney*
The Promise *by R.L. Scott-Buccleuch*
The Man With No Name *by Evelyn Davies and Peter Town*
The Cleverest Person in the World *by Norman Whitney*
Claws *by John Landon*
Z for Zachariah *by Robert C. O'Brien*
Tales of Horror *by Bram Stoker*
Frankenstein *by Mary Shelley*
Silver Blaze and Other Stories *by Sir Arthur Conan Doyle*
Tales of Ten Worlds *by Arthur C. Clarke*
The Boy Who Was Afraid *by Armstrong Sperry*
Room 13 and Other Ghost Stories *by M.R. James*
The Narrow Path *by Francis Selormey*
The Woman in Black *by Susan Hill*

For further information on the full selection of
Readers at all five levels in the series, please refer
to the Heinemann Guided Readers catalogue.

Heinemann English Language Teaching
A division of Heinemann Publishers (Oxford) Ltd
Halley Court, Jordan Hill, Oxford OX2 8EJ

OXFORD MADRID ATHENS PARIS FLORENCE PRAGUE
SÃO PAULO CHICAGO MELBOURNE AUCKLAND
SINGAPORE TOKYO GABORONE
JOHANNESBURG PORTSMOUTH (NH) IBADAN

ISBN 0 435 27215 2

This retold version for Heinemann Guided Readers
© F. H. Cornish 1993
First published 1993

Illustrated by Robert Geary
Typography by Adrian Hodgkins
Designed by Sue Vaudin
Cover by Art Resource and Threefold Design
Typeset in 11.5/14.5 pt Goudy
Printed and bound in Malta by Interprint Limited

95 96 97 10 9 8 7 6 5 4 3